THE LOST SLAYER

Part Two

DARK TIMES

CHRISTOPHER GOLDEN

An original serial novel based on the hit TV series
created by Joss Whedon

POCKET PULSE

New York   London   Toronto   Sydney   Singapore

For information regarding special discounts for bulk purchases, please contact Simon & Schuster Special Sales at 1-800-456-6798 or business@simonandschuster.com

HISTORIAN'S NOTE: This serial story takes place at the beginning of *Buffy*'s fourth season.

An *Original* Publication of POCKET BOOKS

 POCKET PULSE, published by
Pocket Books, a division of Simon & Schuster, Inc.
1230 Avenue of the Americas, New York, NY 10020

™ and © 2001 Twentieth Century Fox Film Corporation. All rights reserved.

ISBN: 0-7434-1186-2

First Pocket Pulse printing September 2001

10 9 8 7 6 5 4 3 2 1

POCKET PULSE and colophon are registered trademarks of Simon & Schuster, Inc.

Printed in the U.S.A.

PROLOGUE

Torn away.

Buffy hurtled forward, not propelled from behind but tugged, dragged, hauled painfully and suddenly into a black and red abyss. It felt as though only her face had been torn away, pulled on farther and farther into the chasm of infinite black before her, but the rest of her left behind, all the weight that flesh and blood and bone added to the image she had of herself. What was she? Mind and heart and soul. Face. Eyes and ears and mouth. Words.

Red whirlpools punctured the endless velvet shadow around her, flashing past as she was dragged by. As if the universe itself were wounded and bleeding.

Vaguely, in the fog that seemed to comprise her mind, a dark certainty overwhelmed her.

This was not a vision. Somehow, her spirit had been torn from her body and was now on a journey. Traveling. Hurtling out of control toward some un-fathomable point in the distance.

Buffy felt her mind slipping away from her, felt her-self shutting down as she was drawn through the void . . . and drawn . . . and drawn. Lulled into a kind of hibernation, aware and yet unresponsive to her surroundings.

Then, suddenly, some sense that the void was not endless, the abyss not infinite. Somewhere ahead was a barrier, a wall, and she was hurtling toward it, bound for collision. She peered into the darkness ahead but all had become black now, as though she were blind. But blind or not, she could feel it, sense its proximity as she was whipped along a course toward inevitable impact.

Collision.

Cold water splashed her face.

Shocked, Buffy stared at her fingers, splayed be-fore her. At the grimy, cracked porcelain of the sink and the water running from the faucet. Instinctively she looked up for a mirror over the sink, but there wasn't one.

Of course there isn't one. They took it away the first day, she thought. She flashed back to that time, five years before, when Clownface and Bulldog had thrown her, beaten, bloody and barely conscious, into this cell for the first time. *They didn't want you to cut your wrists.*

Buffy spun about like a cornered animal, and her eyes darted around the room. The cell. Bars on the two high windows barely allowed the tiniest bit of light from the outside. Ten-foot stone walls all around. A steel door with rivets driven through it and neither handle nor knob nor even keyhole on this side.

Built for me. This was built for me.

Her hands went to the sides of her head and she squeezed her eyes closed. Then she opened them wide and gazed around the room, hugging herself tight. Buffy knew things. She did not know how, but she *knew.*

Impossible.

But inescapably true.

She had been here, in this cell, for a very long time. Reluctantly, afraid of what she would find, she looked at her hands again. Rough, hard hands, with lines that had never been there before. She stretched, felt her body, *looked* at herself.

No thinner than before. But harder. Tighter. Rippled with muscles she remembered seeing in magazines and on television whenever they showed women who were Olympians, whose very life was exercise, exertion, sport.

But there was nothing sporting about this.

Buffy's body was taut and dangerous. She felt it, even in the way she moved. She felt like a weapon.

Gathering dust.

This cell. Endless days and nights alone, with only

these four walls and the ruthless way she forged her body into this steel thing. Vampires with tattooed faces and orange flames in their eyes; they fed her, kept her alive, but nothing more. No talking, not even threats or taunts. Only the toning of her body kept her sane, that focus on the day she would escape.

And in time, even that focus blurred and there was only the routine of exercise. Hope dimmed.

These aren't my memories. Can't be my memories. I remember yesterday. They took Giles. Camazotz is preying on Sunnydale. Lucy Hanover came in my dreams and Willow summoned her and . . .

Buffy stared down at her hands again. And they *were* her hands. Just as the memories of this room— month after month becoming intimate with these four walls, eating the awful slop they fed her, and waiting for an opening—just as those recollections were hers.

Lines on her hands.

Five years since she had been put into this room.

"No," she whispered. *It's impossible.*

"No!" she screamed.

With a roar of fury and hatred surging up from her chest, Buffy ran full tilt at the door. Though her body still felt foreign to her, she loved the way it moved. Fluid and powerful and deadly. She launched a drop kick at the steel door, slammed into it hard enough to rattle her jaw, then fell and banged her head hard on the stone floor. Adrenaline screamed in her, and she pushed the pain away. With a flip, she was up on her feet, and she kicked and punched at the door with only the echo of her own grunts in the room to accompany her.

Several minutes passed. She slowed, breathing heavily.

The adrenaline subsided. The ache in her skull and the pain in her bloody, ravaged knuckles was real. The skin on her fists was scraped raw. Buffy reached up to touch the back of her head, where she'd struck the floor, and her fingers came back streaked with blood.

She would heal quickly. After all, she was the Slayer. But the wounds were real. This was real.

Even as her mind recoiled in horror at these thoughts, even as she examined her body and her surroundings, she felt her memory of the battle with Camazotz begin to dim. Desperate to save Giles, they had summoned Lucy Hanover. Lucy had called upon an entity known only as The Prophet, who promised Buffy a vision of the future, a vision that might help her prevent it and save Giles's life.

The Prophet had touched her.

But this was no vision.

Whatever The Prophet had done, somehow she was not nineteen anymore. Buffy Summers was twenty-four, at least. Maybe twenty-five. Somehow, the entity had torn her spirit from her body that day, years ago, and thrust it into the future, into this body.

Her memories of that day faded, now. Though she

knew in her heart that in some way it had happened only moments before, she remembered it as though years had passed. But there was a blank spot there as well—a period of days she did not remember at all— the time during which she had been captured. A gap in her memory existed between The Prophet touching her and the day when Clownface and Bulldog threw her into her cell.

For more than five years, she had wondered what had happened in that dead space in her memory, that blackout.

No. It isn't me. I haven't been here. It never happened, she reminded herself. And yet there was no longer any doubt that this was real. She could feel every muscle, every scratch, every sensation. This was her own body, her own life, and yet somehow her nineteen-year-old mind had been fast-forwarded into an older body, a dark, horrible future.

And all she could do was pace the cell. Work her body. Train for the day the vampires let their guard down.

Days passed. She trained and slept and washed and trained. They brought food before dawn and after dusk, always armed, always in groups of three or more. Made her stand in the far corner, afraid to have her come too close, as though she were a wild animal.

It made her smile.

Perhaps two weeks later, they brought the girl.

It was dark when they threw her into the cell,

bruised and bloody but conscious. Alive. The girl was a brunette, dark and exotic. *Italian, maybe,* Buffy thought. Tall, but young. Even through the blood, when she looked up with her defiant, crazy eyes, Buffy could see that she was just a kid. Not more than sixteen, maybe younger.

For a moment, Buffy only stood there staring at her, five years without human contact having built up a callus on her heart and soul. She was two people in one, two Buffys at one time, the hardened prisoner and the young warrior. Then suddenly it was as though the part of her mind that was still nineteen simply woke up. It was as though she had been frozen in this body from the moment she had realized what had happened to her.

Now she thawed.

Ice melted away from her true self.

Buffy went to the girl, reached down for her. "Are you all right?"

The girl's eyes changed then. She blinked and her mouth opened with an expression of absolute astonishment.

"Oh my God," the girl whispered, voice cracking. "You're . . . you're her, aren't you?"

"I'm not tracking."

The girl backed away, stood up slowly, painfully, and stared at her. "You're Buffy Summers. I've seen pictures."

"Yeah? How do I look?"

Beaten, bleeding, the girl actually laughed. A discordant sound, but a welcome one just the same. "Like hell," she said. "You look like hell."

"Who are you?" Buffy asked.

But she thought she already knew the answer.

"I'm August."

Buffy frowned. "You're a month?"

"It's my name," the girl said, annoyed. She wiped blood from under her nose but it was still bleeding. "I'm the Slayer now."

Buffy closed her eyes. Shook her head to clear her mind. She felt a little unsteady on her feet. So many questions. But if this girl was a Slayer, what did that mean for—

"Faith?"

August nodded. "Six months ago. They tried for years to catch her, the way they . . . the way they did you. If it weren't for her they'd have the whole West Coast by now, maybe more. At least that's what my Watcher says. They caught her outside of L.A., I heard."

Wary, maybe even a little afraid, the girl gave Buffy a cautious look. "Have you been here all along? All this time?"

No. I just got here. A couple of weeks ago. I'm not supposed to be here. Those were the first thoughts in her head, but even as they flickered through her mind she knew they weren't really true.

"All this time," Buffy told her. She turned her back on the girl and began to pace the room. "And now I've got company."

"But haven't you tried to—"

Buffy spun to face her, nearly growling. "Every day. What the hell do you think I am? I'm the Slayer."

"You're *a* Slayer," August corrected. "Not even the main one anymore. Not for a long time. The Council, they just call you the Lost Slayer now. Not even your name."

Buffy took that in. In her mind she reached back to the moment she knew was truly hers, where her mind belonged. Her soul . . . where her soul had been pushed away, into the here and now, and her body left behind. Hijacked.

What had happened between then and now? Where were they all? What had happened to Giles?

"How much territory do they control? Camazotz and the vampires?" she asked.

August seemed deeply troubled. She stared at the steel door, then turned back to look at Buffy, sizing her up.

"Well?" Buffy prodded.

"Sunnydale. A few other towns. Maybe a thirty mile radius around."

"And nobody knows?"

"Nobody believes," August told her. "Nobody wants to believe. That's how they win. Spin control. Marketing the illusion that everything's normal. Plenty of humans willing to help for a piece of the power."

"God," Buffy rasped.

"So there's no way out of here?" August asked, her voice taking on a kind of quiet desperation, as if she

CITY COLLEGE

had surrendered a part of herself. "You've tried everything?"

"Five years is a long time," Buffy told her. "Maybe with two of us now it'll be different, but I figure they'll just send more guards now to bring the meals."

"Then I guess we don't have any choice," August said softly. Her eyes filled with moisture and she wiped at them bitterly. Then she took a breath and steadied herself, a grim expression on her face.

"Again, not tracking," Buffy told her.

August stared at her as though she were stupid. "They captured you because they finally got smart. If you don't kill the Slayer, there won't be another one. Keep you in here . . ." she whirled around, threw her arms up in near hysteria. "Keep us in here, and there'll never be another Slayer."

Buffy stared at her. "You have a gift for stating the obvious."

"You're just going to let them? There's nothing to stop them from spreading even further now." August bit her lip, shook her head and hugged herself as though attempting to deny the thoughts that were filling her head.

"It sucks. It truly does," Buffy said, hearing the pain in her own voice. The despair. "But until they get careless, and let down their guard, there's nothing we can do."

August pushed a lock of her dark hair behind her ears. She would not turn her iron-gray eyes up to look at Buffy.

"There's something I can do," she said softly.

One eyebrow raised, Buffy studied her. "What's that? What can you do?"

Finally, August met her gaze. Her soft eyes had hardened again. Crazy, defiant eyes. Eyes cold and decisive.

"I can kill you."

CHAPTER 1

I can kill you.

The stone walls of the cell echoed back the words, and then silence descended. No noise came from the corridor beyond the steel door. The only thing Buffy Summers could hear was her own gentle breathing, and that of the sixteen-year-old girl standing across from her. The one who had spoken those impossible words.

Buffy tensed, taut muscles bunched, and she rose on the balls of her feet. Five years she had been in this fifteen-foot square, a chamber of rock and metal constructed with the express purpose of keeping her within. Five years she had honed her body until it was a coiled spring, a scalpel, a bullwhip . . . all of that and more. When the vampires came to bring food or clothing or bedding, they came in force, with stun guns, and they used them. In all the times she had tried to escape and failed, all the dreams she had had of combat, never had she imagined that the next threat she would face would come from another Slayer.

The girl, August, sensed the alarm in Buffy, and her stance altered slightly, subtly. Though younger, the dark-haired girl was taller than Buffy, and likely thought that an advantage.

"You're not thinking clearly," Buffy said, a rasp in her voice. She had used it so little in recent years.

August seemed to quiver, almost humming with energy like a high-tension wire. Her tongue snaked out and wetted her lips. "My thinking is perfectly clear, Summers. It's your head that's not screwed on straight here. Look around. You're a zoo animal. They've kept you like a tiger in a cage, and you've *let* them."

Again, her words echoed off cold stone. The two young women began, slowly, to move, to circle, eyeing one another, looking for vulnerabilities. In the back of her mind, a voice shouted for Buffy to stop this madness, not to let it happen. It was the voice of her younger self, somehow implanted within this twenty-four-year-old body. But the two minds were both *her,* and so they had begun to merge. The two were one. Despite the reluctance she felt, Buffy knew that only a fool would leave herself open to attack.

It was simple caution for her to be wary of August's threat. The girl, the young Slayer, had a desperation in her eyes that said she might do anything.

"For more than three years, I tried to escape every time the door was opened," Buffy said. "They took to stunning me on principle. After a while I decided to study them instead, try to figure out the psychology of my jailers. Within six months I knew them all, their vulnerabilities, what would work to distract them. Just from listening and watching. Two days before I planned to make my escape, they were all replaced. Someone knew. Someone understood what I was doing."

"Exactly my point," August said grimly. She shook her hands out as she glared at Buffy. "You're a pet. Your master knows you too well."

Buffy froze. "I don't have a master."

"Look around. They might as well have one of those little hamster wheels in here. Or a Habitrail."

Buffy stepped slightly back from August and kept the girl in her peripheral vision, then did indeed look around. Though the room was cold stone, there were several throw rugs on the floor. A plastic rack upon which were piled the blue jeans, white tanks, and sweatshirts they supplied her with; all U.C. Sunnydale sweatshirts, which were all the vampires would give her. Some kind of joke, she was sure. There was her metal-framed bed—all welded to keep her from using part of it as a weapon, and a steel table bolted to the floor. Nothing wood, of course, for wood could splinter, and splintered wood could kill her captors.

"I don't see what you see. They need me alive," Buffy said. "Food and water, clothing."

August shook her head. The expression on her face might have been called a sneer if not for the sadness in it.

"All this time, though. If you realized that you couldn't escape, you could have found a way to force them to kill you. Could have killed yourself, if that didn't work. Shatter that porcelain sink, use it to slash your wrists, bleed out here on the floor. But you didn't. Why didn't you?"

Buffy shook her head. *"That's* your solution? What's the Council teaching you? I'm the Slayer. Once I get out, there'll be hell to pay."

Though she had been on guard, the absurdity of August's rantings had caused Buffy to pause for a moment in surprise.

August moved. With a single, fluid motion, so fast Buffy barely had time to react, she stepped into the space between them and lashed out with a savage backhand. The blow struck Buffy's cheek hard, but she rolled with it, turned in an instant and readied herself for another attack.

None came.

Instead, August only stood and stared at her, face reddened with rage. Tears began to stream down her face.

"How can you be so arrogant?" August demanded. A lock of her hair had fallen across her eyes but she did not move it. "You're *a* Slayer, not *the* Slayer. You're not what's important. The only thing that matters is that there be someone out there to fight them.

Once you get out, there'll be hell to pay? That's what you said. It's *already* hell out there, Summers. Can you help them?"

A chill seemed to weave frozen tendrils all through Buffy's body. Though the idea horrified her—everything August was suggesting did—there was a kind of blunt, primitive truth to it as well. Was it arrogant of her to think she was more valuable alive than dead? Simply by staying alive, she had given her captors what they wanted. Yet the idea of doing anything else . . .

She shook her head. "No. Listen. Now that we're both in here, we'll find a way. Before they figure out what it takes to contain us both."

August laughed bitterly and wiped away a tear. "You've been here five years! We can't get out, Buffy. The only way for there to be a new Slayer, out there, fighting the darkness, is for one of us to die. If you're not willing to do what has to be done . . . I will."

The dry shuffle of their feet upon the stone floor was an eerie whisper. The two Slayers began to circle again, and though she rejected the very idea of what was happening, Buffy could not deny it. It was a dark, vicious irony, a nightmare made real. Her throat was dry, but she felt the power in her body, tendons and muscles moving with grace and precision.

"I won't kill you, August. But I'm not going to let you kill me, either."

The girl's face darkened further. Fresh tears sprang to her cheeks. The teenager beneath the Slayer's façade was revealed.

"Damn you!" August cried, the words heavy with the weight of her pain and grief. "Do you think I want this? I've got people I love out there. Dying every day, trying to keep the vampires from spreading. Someone's got to protect them."

"We'll find a way. It may take a little time—"

But the conversation was over. August glared at her coldly, now, and wiped the last tear from her red-rimmed eyes. Her lips were pressed together in anguish, and she shuddered once, then was still. The girl dropped into a battle stance that Buffy was all too familiar with. It had been the first one Giles had taught her when he took over as her Watcher.

"August—"

"Quiet," the girl snapped.

August leaped at her in a spinning kick aimed directly at her head. Though Buffy saw it coming, had been prepared for it, it was only instinct that saved her from the blow. She darted her head to the side, dodged the kick by a scant half-inch. With her right hand, she caught August's ankle and reversed the direction of the kick, spinning the girl onto the floor. August's shoulder struck the stone hard, but even as Buffy moved in on her, the girl rolled, swung her foot out and swept Buffy's legs out from under her.

Even as she fell, Buffy spun and threw her body forward. She ducked her head, went into a roll that took her across the room, then leaped to her feet only inches shy of her bed.

August was already there. As Buffy came up, the

younger Slayer snapped a side kick at her chest. Buffy could not avoid it. Something in her chest cracked and all the breath went from her lungs. She crashed into the plastic shelving holding her clothes and it splintered and broke apart beneath her.

Her rib cage grated painfully as she moved, but Buffy rolled up against the wall, amidst the wreckage of the shelves. A shard of plastic pierced her side, but she ignored the lancing pain, so superficial compared to the burning in her chest when she breathed.

Mouth still set in that grim line, eyes red with tears fallen and unfallen, August went for a simple kick. Buffy had counted on her believing that her chest injury had caused her to cower against the wall to make herself less vulnerable. August was young. She bought it.

With an open hand, she stopped the kick mid-swing and shoved August backward. Braced against the wall, Buffy had enough support to knock her off her feet. With the enhanced strength of the Slayer, she pushed the younger Slayer with such force that August flailed at the air, unable to spin out of the fall. Her head struck the edge of the steel table as she went down.

Though she pushed herself up on her hands and knees, August was too slow, too vulnerable.

Buffy was up, frustrated, searching for some way to stop this fight before it ended the way August wanted it to.

She was stronger than this girl. Probably faster as well. August had been Slayer for six months, maybe trained for a year or two before that. Buffy had been the Slayer more than three years before she was captured and had worked her body mercilessly in the interim, not merely with exercise, but with shadow-boxing and a martial arts *kata* she had devised from the various disciplines she had studied before.

But she was trying to reason with a girl on the brink of madness, a Slayer driven past rationality by the world she lived in. It disturbed Buffy deeply to think how desperate things must be to drive August to this.

Not that it mattered, now.

The girl wanted to kill her. In order to prevent that, to reason with her, she would have to incapacitate the younger Slayer, at the very least.

She watched August warily, her eyes wide, imploring. "It shouldn't be like this."

August shook off the blow to her head. She would not raise her eyes to look at Buffy, only crouched there for a moment on hands and knees.

"No. It shouldn't," she agreed. "But it is."

Silent, lightning fast, August shot up from the floor and barreled into Buffy. It was a brute's move, with no finesse, no precision, but it worked. August used her greater height and weight to ram Buffy up against the stone wall. The impact drove the air from Buffy's lungs again, and the fire of pain in her chest from her cracked ribs flared even more brightly.

August snapped her open hand forward in a palm strike that drove into Buffy's shoulder quite precisely, dislocating it with a loud pop and an agonizing tear. Black spots clouded Buffy's vision, but she knew that was just the pain.

Pain was an old and familiar friend, by now.

It woke her up.

It pissed her off.

But before she could react, August gave her a quick shot to the face. Her nose broke and blood began to flow.

The next blow never touched her. Buffy dodged and August's fist hit the stone wall. Something in her hand broke with an audible snap, but August only grunted softly.

"That's it. You don't get any more free shots," Buffy snarled.

The copper tang of blood touched her lips, her dislocated arm hung loosely at her side, but Buffy popped August with a head-butt. Stunned, August staggered back. She cradled her right fist, then tried to spin up into a high kick.

Buffy ducked in, slammed her palm into August's upper chest, and knocked her down. The gash in her side did not slow her, nor did her dislocated shoulder or her broken nose.

"Get up," Buffy told her. "Stop this. If I have to, I'll break both your arms, but I don't want to have to feed you for the next few months."

August glared at her, beyond reason. The crazed girl leaped up again, back into a battle stance, despite her shattered fist.

"Damn you," Buffy whispered.

With a cry of anguish, August launched a blow with her good hand. Buffy dodged, but the girl followed through, stepped into her blow, past Buffy, then brought her arm back and shot an elbow at the back of Buffy's head.

Furious, Buffy stumbled forward and then turned to see August lunging at her again. The steel table was behind her. Buffy hopped up on top of it, avoiding August's attack. Then she kicked out at the girl's damaged hand and August shrieked with pain and staggered back.

Tears sprang to August's face again. She stood for a moment, panting, glaring at Buffy. "They need us, don't you get it?"

"Not like this," Buffy said softly. "Not like this."

"I won't stop," August vowed. "One of us is going to die."

Buffy only shook her head in denial and clutched her dislocated arm against her body.

August rushed the table. Buffy dove into the air, executed a somersault over the girl's head and landed on both feet. In one fluid motion, she shot a hard kick up at the younger Slayer's head. August tried to dodge. She was a scant heartbeat too slow.

There was no time for Buffy to even try to abort the attack. The kick caught the other girl in the side of the neck, just where her jaw met her neck. With a wet snap, her spinal column broke right at the top, and her corpse tumbled backward with the force of the kick and rolled in a heap across the stone floor.

August did not move, not even a twitch. Buffy knew she was dead.

"Oh God, no," Buffy whispered.

Hot tears came into her eyes, but her grief was quickly overcome by anger. "Dammit, no!" she shouted. "No! No! No!"

With her good hand she covered her eyes, spun around in a small circle. It *was* a nightmare. It *had* to be. But the raging pain in her shoulder and the copper taste of her own blood on her lips, was real.

The girl in front of her, August, a Slayer, was dead. That was real.

"How?" she whispered. "It wasn't supposed to be like this. Stupid girl . . ."

But she was not sure if that last part was meant to be addressed to August or to herself. It was cruel, without doubt. All this time alone, then finally contact with not just another human being, but a person who was part of the same mission. And now this.

Her tears felt cold on her cheeks compared to the heat of her blood. Buffy knelt by August and pushed a lock of her hair away from her fine, Italian features, and just studied her for a moment. She wondered if she herself had ever looked so young.

New hatred welled up within her, bearing a razor edge sharper than anything she had felt in years. They had taken Giles from her, Camazotz and his vampire hordes. They had imprisoned her. But they had never been able to take even a sliver of her hope and her faith.

Until now.

Teeth gritted together, a violent surge of adrenaline making Buffy bounce slightly on her feet. She used her good hand to drag August around near the front of the cell, only inches from the door. It would hit her when it opened.

Where August's corpse had lain, she knelt, took a breath, and whacked her broken nose with an open hand. She let the cry of pain come, and sagged a bit. Then she bent over and let blood flow onto the floor. After a couple of minutes, she rolled up the back of her shirt and felt for the puncture wound left in her side by the broken plastic that had impaled her. The wound had already begun to heal.

Buffy used her fingernail to dig it open.

Again, she bled.

But the loss of blood did not weaken her. For it was not her own lifeblood that drove her now, but hatred for her enemy, like nothing she had ever felt before. Her world had been gray for so long that she could remember almost nothing else. Gray and numb and lifeless.

It had color again. The world was crimson as her blood, and black as a vampire's heart.

She allowed herself only one more minute to recover, to breathe slowly. Then she stood and went to the sink, still cradling her dislocated arm. She sat on the floor. With some difficulty, she managed to wrap both hands around the pipe that came down from beneath the sink. Strong hand over the weak one, holding it in place, she planted her feet against the wall under the sink, took a breath, and pushed out as hard as she could.

An awkward angle, but there was enough force behind it to snap the shoulder back into the joint. It felt as though someone were trying to separate the bones with a jagged knife. Buffy could have stopped the scream by biting through her lip. She did not.

Her mouth opened and she shrieked loud and long, releasing all the pain and misery she had been holding inside. Somehow she managed to find her feet and stumbled to the shattered plastic shelving. She snatched up a splintered piece, brought it to her flesh, and sliced a long, clean, horizontal cut across her throat.

Buffy hissed air in through her clenched teeth, for the cut stung, but it was superficial. Nothing vital was hit. After her shoulder, it was almost nothing.

Quivering from the pain and her emotional turmoil, she staggered to the place where she had made herself bleed. A small pool of her blood was there on the stone. Not enough, to her eyes, but it would have to do.

She dropped the plastic dagger to the floor a foot away, then lay down on her side, right cheek already sticky where it touched the edge of the puddle of her blood.

Maddox stormed down the corridor with a cigarette clenched firmly in his lips and a two foot stunprod gripped in his right hand. One of the guards—a rookie named Theo who was practically a newborn—followed behind him like a puppy.

"Whaddaya think's goin' on, Maddox?" Theo cooed excitedly. "There were screams and everything.

Sounded pretty nasty. Got a serious Slayer catfight, I think. Woulda loved to've seen that."

"We'll see."

They rounded a corner and Maddox saw four other guards up ahead, the two who were supposed to be on the door, and two others who had likely come down from the upper level when the commotion began.

"What the hell's going on?" Maddox demanded.

"Told you, Maddox," Theo said, grinning. "They're tearing each other apart in there. When you said put the new girl in there, that's the last thing I expected."

With a grunt, Maddox froze. He turned to stare at Theo. "Who sired you?"

Theo blinked. "Um, Harmony did."

Maddox sighed. "Of course she did."

Then he tapped Theo's chest lightly with the stun-prod. The vampire jerked and shuddered as electricity surged through him. His eyes were wide, white against the black tattoo Maddox thought he brought shame to. Theo slumped to the ground, jerking a bit. He opened his mouth and a tiny bit of bloody drool spilled out with the tip of his tongue, which he had bitten off.

With a sigh, Maddox turned to the four guards. They were proper vampires, eyes crackling orange, grim-faced, not at all perturbed by what they had seen. Or, at least, not revealing it if they were.

"Remind me to kill Harmony," he said.

The others all nodded, once, silently.

"You're ready?"

Each of them unsnapped a prod similar to the one Maddox held, only smaller and more portable. Maddox could smell the blood inside the room, the scent seeping beneath the steel door. It worried him. He was responsible for what happened within that cell.

Anxious, he gestured to the guards. "Open the door."

The one in front, Brossi, glanced once at Maddox. Other than Maddox, he was the only one who had been there from the beginning. The two of them had been part of the group that had captured Buffy Summers in the first place. They knew what she was capable of.

The door itself was testament to that. There were three locks, equidistant from one another. Each controlled an inch-thick iron deadbolt that, when engaged, locked into a metal casing that itself was plugged into the center of the three-foot-thick stone wall that framed the door. There were two more deadbolts each at the top and bottom of the door, though these had no locks.

It took Brossi a few seconds to unlock the door, then disengage the three main bolts. He hesitated for a moment, turned to glance at Maddox, and then his face changed, forehead erupting into the brutal guise of the vampire. His fangs lengthened and he ran his tongue over them.

Maddox had more control than that, but he did not blame Brossi for feeling threatened. Every time they opened that door, twice a day, they had to be prepared for a fight. Just when they thought Summers was beaten into submission, that was when she was most likely to attack again. When he had been instructed to put the new girl into the same cell, Maddox had balked. It was just asking for trouble. No question it was going to make feeding time even more difficult.

But this was the last thing he had expected.

"Careful," Maddox told the guards.

Brossi slammed back the bolts on the top and bottom of the door, sliding them abruptly out of their metal casings. There was no way to do it quietly, so he opted to do it quickly. The other guards with their stun-prods gathered behind him, tattooed faces expressionless, only the glittering fire of their eyes giving away their anxiety. Maddox stepped up behind them, but at a respectful distance. It was not that he was a coward. Quite the opposite, in fact. If this was some sham and the two Slayers killed them all, it would fall to him to stop them.

"Go!" Maddox ordered.

Brossi shoved the door open with his shoulder, tensed for an attack. The steel door swung eight or nine inches, then hit an obstruction with a dull thump. The vampire guard took a half-step back and prepared to defend himself. Nothing happened, and after a moment, he pushed at the door again, put his weight behind it, and it opened slowly as the obstruction slid out of the way.

"What the hell is that?" Maddox asked, trying to see over the shoulders of the guards.

Half inside the door, Brossi glanced back quickly. "The new girl. She's down."

Cursing loudly, Maddox shoved the others aside and moved up behind Brossi. It was his job not just to keep the Slayers prisoner, but to keep them alive. Maddox peered over Brossi's shoulder, trying to see deeper into the room to make certain Summers wasn't lying in wait. Then he turned and glared at the guards around him.

"Stay back. Either one of them makes it to the door, take her. Break something, burn something, whatever, but I don't have to tell you what will happen if any of you kill one of them."

He gave Brossi a nudge. "Stun her."

Maddox's gaze ticked down to the still form of the teenaged Slayer on the floor, then back at the room. The door was still only partially open, and he could not see Summers anywhere.

She's there, though. A frisson of fear went through him. There was something about the woman that had always given him the creeps a little bit. She was warm and soft, like all humans, and yet there was something almost haunting about her, almost mystical. There was a promise in her eyes every time she looked at him; a promise of payback.

Brossi extended his arm through the open door, stun-prod in hand. Maddox stood back a little, just in case the door should be slammed shut suddenly, his own electrical prod held up at the ready.

As Maddox watched, Brossi tagged the downed Slayer with the prod. Electricity sizzled through her with a crackle and the smell of sizzling hair. The girl did not so much as twitch. There were none of the muscle spasms that electrocution brought.

"Dammit," Maddox whispered. *I'm screwed.*

The girl looked badly beaten. There had been a knock-down, drag-out brawl inside that cell. One Slayer was dead. But what of the other one?

"I'm coming in, Summers. Keep away from the door!" he called into the cell.

Then he motioned Brossi out of the way and kicked the door with all the strength he could muster. Something broke in the corpse on the floor when the door collided with it, but it slid open another half-foot.

Just enough for Maddox to see Buffy Summers lying in a pool of her own blood, bruised and beaten, throat slit, eyes wide and cold and staring right at him.

"No!" Maddox screamed. He struck out at the air, then rammed a fist against the door with a clang and did not even feel the pain. "Dammit, no!"

Furious, and filled with terror as he began to wonder what fate awaited him now, Maddox strode into the room. His stun-prod hung at his side. Astonished, he stared around at the shattered plastic shelving, the clothes strewn about. From a distance, he examined the splintered piece of plastic that had obviously been used to slash Buffy's throat.

"Maddox, how . . .?" Brossi began to ask.

His words trailed off when Maddox glared at him. "New girl cut Summers's throat. Summers broke her neck before she died."

"I don't know," Brossi said slowly. "Better keep back from her. Give her a few volts before you get too close."

Maddox hesitated. Then he studied the Slayer's eyes, the haunting eyes that had promised him death so many times. There was nothing there now. Like tarnished marbles, they were.

The way she lay, mouth partially open, the blood from the wound in her throat had pooled up against her lips. That was the thing that convinced Maddox. That whole side of her face, her hair, her nose, lay in blood, and with her mouth open like that, if she were alive, well . . . she would have been able to taste it. Her own blood. Like a vampire.

Her chest did not move. Her eyes were dead ice fragments. But it was that one detail that convinced him.

Still, Maddox was cautious as he reached out with the stun-prod. The eyes still gave him a chill. The tip of the prod swept toward the woman's eyes, but there wasn't so much as a flinch. Just for safety's sake, he touched the prod against her shoulder. The body jerked slightly, but he'd seen that before. The electricity that surged through the corpse was enough to do that. The hair on the dead woman's head shivered and even floated a bit with the static.

"She's dead," Maddox said, forlorn. "What the hell do I do now?"

He was about to prod her eyes when a thought

occurred to him. Maddox turned and looked at Brossi.

"Or is she?" he said, grinning. "I mean, *he* never comes here, right? We'll just lock it up again, leave them here."

Brossi's expression was grave. "When the new Slayer shows up, he'll know."

"We could be gone by then," Maddox replied sharply. "It's a big world."

Brossi hung his head, all the tension going out of him. In the corridor, the other guards were wide-eyed with the realization of their fate. One of them, Haskell, cut and ran right then, his footsteps echoing back down the corridor. For a moment, Brossi turned in that direction, then regarded Maddox again.

"There isn't anywhere far enough," he said. "It's over, Maddox."

"I never even wanted this job!" Maddox shouted, his voice echoing in the cell.

Mind spinning, he turned back toward Summers again. Rage and fear building inside him, Maddox swung back his leg to kick the corpse. His boot thunked into her flesh . . . *moving* flesh. As if it were part of his own motion, she closed herself around his leg, crawling halfway up it, and snapped it at the knee.

Maddox screamed.

As he went down, he felt the prod tugged from his grasp, and then Buffy Summers, the Slayer, stood over him, her resurrection as sudden as a vampire's, but far more shocking to him.

Despite the pain of his shattered leg, he grinned. She wasn't dead.

"Maddox!" Brossi shouted.

"Don't kill her!" Maddox roared.

The other guards, against his previous orders, began to enter the cell. They all seemed to be moving in slow motion in comparison to the Slayer, and each had a kind of vacant, frightened look in his eyes. He did not blame them. Summers had only ever been a captive to them, but in all that time, they had never underestimated how dangerous she was.

Once upon a time, Camazotz had kept the existence of the Slayer hidden from his Kakchiquels, but that had changed after her capture. They had all heard tales of the Slayers now, and knew that Summers was among the most dangerous who had ever lived. For their entire community, the girl locked in this custom dungeon had become almost mythical.

Now they had seen her dead. She had taken a hit from the prod and barely reacted. She had lost a great deal of blood. It was almost as though what they fought was a horrible specter of the Slayer, rather than mere flesh and blood. Not a woman, but a bogeyman so terrible even the creatures of darkness feared her.

They had barely kept her caged all this time.

And now she had a weapon.

In the dim light of the stone room, Maddox

reached out for the metal table and struggled to rise. The Slayer moved so fast he could barely keep his eyes on her. All in all, it would have been much better if she had had a stake. Brossi was electrocuted and then decapitated. The other two were disarmed before she broke them. Maddox could only watch.

Then she came for him.